Disney

The ARISTOKITTENS

The Fantastic
Rabbit Race

The Aristokittens

Welcome to the Creature Café
The Great Biscuit Bake-Off

The Fantastic
Rabbit Race

By Jennifer Castle

Illustrated by Sydney Hanson

𝒟ISNEY PRESS

Los Angeles • New York

Printed in the United States of America

First Paperback Edition, October 2022

First Hardcover Edition, October 2022

1 3 5 7 9 10 8 6 4 2

ISBN 978-1-368-06804-8 (Paperback), ISBN 978-1-368-06974-8 (Hardcover)

FAC-004510-22245

Library of Congress Control Number: 2022930835

Book design by Catalina Castro

Visit disneybooks.com

Chapter 1

Berlioz the kitten licked his right front paw. Then he licked it again, and again, until it felt exactly as clean as the left one.

He glanced around him, noticing how busy things were at the Purrfect Paw-tisserie, the Paris creature café he ran with his brother, Toulouse, and sister, Marie. Many of the animals coming in to try their kitty croissants or new dog treats were ones he'd never seen before.

The door to the alley outside opened again, and three birds fluttered in.

"Wow, our first blackbird guests!" Berlioz said to himself as he watched them scramble toward the pastry case. They pecked at the glass to show Toulouse, who was serving customers, what they wanted. Berlioz had been trying to spread news about the café to more animals, and it must have been working! Now it was time to entertain all these new faces.

He swept his fluffy gray tail out behind him and sat down on the stool in front of his piano.

"Do you really still need the tail-sweep?" someone asked from behind him.

Berlioz spun around on the stool

to see Marie, her fur the color of fresh white snow, watching him with curiosity.

"Of course," Berlioz replied. "Mama taught me three reminders to give myself when I'm getting ready to perform. Number one: sweep your tail out behind you so you don't sit on it by accident."

"I remember," Marie said, rolling her big blue eyes. Then she pointed with a paw to the pink bow around her neck.

"Number two: make sure your bow is straight and tight." Berlioz felt his own bow, a red one, and nodded. "Check," he said.

"Hmmm, I can't remember the third one," Marie murmured, thinking hard as she thumped her tail on the floor.

Berlioz smiled. He loved it when he knew more than his sister. "Stretch out your fingers one by one, but not your claws, because nobody likes scratched piano keys."

Then he did just that, making sure each finger stretch made a satisfying *crack*.

Marie gave an exasperated sigh. "Are you finally ready?"

"One more thing," Berlioz replied. "Lately, I've been giving myself a fourth

 4

reminder: relax and have fun! It's important when you're playing jazz."

"No jazz until we sing the 'Purrfect Paw-tisserie' song," Marie said. "It's a crowd favorite."

"You mean it's *your* favorite, but sure," Berlioz replied playfully. "Let's sing the chorus together this time, okay?"

Marie smiled. "Okay!"

Berlioz's new reminder to *relax and have fun* really came in handy now that Marie was taking breaks from baking to perform with him. He was still getting used to sharing the spotlight.

Together, they entertained their customers with a tune Berlioz had written when they first opened the

café. Their voices blended in perfect
harmony, and many of the animals knew
the song so well, they mouthed along
as Berlioz and Marie wrapped up their
performance:

> *We kittens worked together to bring*
>   *YOU all together*
> *And now that you're here, we'll let*
>   *out a cheer*
> *For food and art and song*
> *And everyone getting along*
> *At the Purrfect Paw-tisserie!*

After the applause died down, a
high-pitched voice squealed out from
somewhere in the café. "Oh, oh, oh!
Love your bunny ears! And yours! And

yours! Did you make them? Can I have one? Please, please, please?"

Berlioz whirled around to see his squirrel friend, Pouf, who lived in the park across the street. Pouf flicked his super-fluffy tail in all directions as he chattered at the three blackbirds.

"Ooh, I want a pair, too!" a chipmunk customer said. "Do you have them in extra-extra-small?"

"We just made these for ourselves," one of the blackbirds replied. "But we can teach you how to create your own."

Berlioz looked more closely and noticed that each blackbird was wearing a hat made of twigs, straw, and grass— almost like they had made a nest, but in the shape of bunny ears.

 7

Now all the other animals in the café were gathering around the blackbirds, oohing and aahing over these bunny ear hats.

"What in the whiskers is going on over there?" Marie asked Berlioz.

"I have no idea," Berlioz replied. "Let's ask Pierre."

They went to find their friend Pierre, a French bulldog who helped them with the café and lived upstairs with his human family. He and Toulouse were arranging dog treats on a tray in the pastry case. When Marie pointed out the blackbirds, Pierre took one look and said, "*Bah!* It must be time for the Fantastic Rabbit Race."

"The Fantastic What-y What?" Berlioz asked.

"Every year, the rabbit community holds a secret race right here in Paris," Pierre explained. "It's a big obstacle course through the Luxembourg Gardens. Rabbits come from all over the globe to compete."

Pouf the squirrel heard them talking and scrambled over. "The Fantastic Rabbit Race is the best! The most fun! The most exciting animal event EVER! This year I'm rooting for Angelique! She's from Paris! And she's terrific! Amazing! Incredible!"

"Ah yes, I've heard about Angelique," Pierre said. "She grew up racing through the city's backyards and gardens, right? This is her first time running the Fantastic Rabbit Race. I would love to see her win, especially after last year."

"Oh, yes!" Pouf agreed, nodding his little head up and down. "Last year was awful! Terrible!"

Berlioz's eyes widened. "What happened last year?"

"There was a champion racer named Edward Earsworth," Pierre said. "He was so fast, with a winning streak of five Fantastic Rabbit Races in a row. But then, during last year's race, he got caught *cheating*. Now he's banned forever."

"Sneaky bunny!" Pouf added. "Bad! Naughty!"

A loud squawk suddenly echoed through the café. Berlioz glanced up to see one of the blackbirds angrily flapping its wings at the chipmunk, which now had a berry stuffed in its cheek.

"You stole that from my bunny ear hat!" the blackbird shouted at the chipmunk.

"No, it fell off your hat and landed on the floor!" the chipmunk replied.

The blackbird flapped its wings even more angrily at the chipmunk, and the chipmunk chattered back at the blackbird.

The fur on Berlioz's back stood on end.

"Hey!" Berlioz whispered to his brother and sister. "That blackbird shouldn't just accuse someone of stealing like that."

He took a step toward the blackbird

and chipmunk, but Toulouse grabbed his tail with both paws.

"No, it's the chipmunk who did something wrong!" Toulouse said. "He should have given the berry back to the bird!"

Berlioz batted his brother away, but when he turned back, Pierre was standing in between them.

"What are you doing, Pierre?"
Berlioz mewed. "Let us through!"

"We should try to fix that fight,"
Toulouse added.

"No you shouldn't," Pierre said.
"First of all, you don't actually know
what happened. Second, as the owners
of this café, you should never take sides
when it comes to disagreements between
the customers. It's not good for business!"

Berlioz glanced at Marie and
Toulouse, who looked back at him with
expressions that said, *I hate to admit it, but
Pierre is right.*

"Okay," Berlioz said with a sigh. "It's
true, we don't have all the information.
But I still think we could help them
somehow."

"You can ask them to drop the

argument or continue it outside," Pierre said. "Watch."

Pierre approached the blackbird and the chipmunk, whispering sternly to them. The two customers exchanged one last glare at each other, then went off in different directions.

"Phew," Toulouse said. "That's a relief."

"I still think that blackbird was being unfair," Berlioz muttered to himself.

Suddenly, the door to the café swung open. Something small and brown streaked through it and around one table, then underneath another. When it stopped in front of the pastry case, Berlioz could see that it was a tiny squirrel.

"Good morning!" the squirrel squeaked at the kittens. "I've been sent to pick up a dozen carrot mini muffins for a rabbit racer!"

"A dozen?" Marie exclaimed with surprise.

"Yes! I told Angelique how delicious your muffins are! And she's hungry! Starving!"

"Wait," Toulouse said. "The order is for Angelique?"

"Yes!" the squirrel said, hopping up and down with impatience. "She's practicing in the park right now!"

Toulouse turned to Marie. "Good thing we just baked a batch of carrot mini muffins this morning."

"Can I take them over to her?" Berlioz asked his littermates. "I'd love to meet Angelique!"

Marie flicked her tail. "Berlioz, I thought we were going to perform all afternoon! Besides, what if there are other racers there? They may think we're rooting for her. If they do that, they might not come to the café."

Pierre laughed. "Now you're thinking like a businesscat, Marie." The French bulldog ducked into the pastry case, took out a tray of carrot muffins, and started to put some in a bag.

"I can deliver them," the squirrel offered, then turned to Berlioz. "I can also show you the track, if you want to meet some of the racers."

"Thank you!" Berlioz exclaimed, then turned to Pierre. "That's not taking sides, right?"

"Not at all," Pierre replied. "It sounds like an invitation you shouldn't pass up."

"We'd like to go, too!" Marie and Toulouse both cried.

"Go, have fun," Pierre said with a wave of his paw. "I'll watch the café."

"Pouf, would you like to come with us?" Berlioz asked their squirrel friend.

Pouf nodded, his tail dancing with excitement.

As the three kittens and two squirrels headed for the café door, Marie turned to Berlioz.

"We're still going to perform some more songs when we get back, right?" she asked. "I want to do a solo."

"Sure," Berlioz said with a sigh. As his littermates sped up ahead of him, he repeated that new reminder to himself.

Relax and have fun.

Hopefully, with a special tour of the Rabbit Race grounds, the *fun* part would be easy.

Chapter 2

The little gray squirrel led Berlioz, Marie, Toulouse, and Pouf down the alley, across a bustling Paris street, and into the Luxembourg Gardens. As they made their way toward a far corner of the park, Pouf spouted trivia facts about the Fantastic Rabbit Race:

"They hold the race here in Paris every year, but the course is different each time!"

"There's always lots of obstacles that the rabbits have to climb or jump over!"

"Sometimes there's a maze! One year, a rabbit from Greece got lost in it and didn't come out until three days later!"

"The racecourse is over there!" the gray squirrel called out, pointing toward a thicket of trees. "Follow me!"

He led the kittens into the thicket. When they came out the other side, they saw rabbits *everywhere*. Rabbits of all sizes, all types, and all colors.

Most of the rabbits were gathered in groups, but there was one rabbit standing by herself, brushing dirt off her feet. She was tall with sleek brown fur, long ears, and even longer legs.

"Oh my gosh!" Pouf exclaimed when he saw the brown rabbit. "That's her! That's Angelique! She's right there!"

Pouf turned and scampered up the nearest tree, perching on a branch above them.

"What are you doing?" Berlioz asked him.

"I'm shy!" Pouf replied.

The other, small squirrel rushed up to Angelique, dropped the bag of muffins at her feet, and darted away. Dozens of other rabbits glanced over to see what was happening.

"See," Marie said, nudging Berlioz. "It's better that we're not the ones delivering the muffins."

"Maybe," Berlioz grumbled. "But I still want to meet her."

They watched Angelique as she pulled a carrot muffin out of the bag and took a huge bite. Then another . . . and in a snap, she'd gobbled up the whole thing.

"Then meet her," Toulouse said, nudging his brother forward with his nose. "Don't chicken out now."

"H-h-hello, Angelique," Berlioz said nervously. "I'm Berlioz. These are my littermates, Toulouse and Marie."

Angelique swallowed her final bite of muffin and broke into a huge, warm smile. Her bright brown eyes sparkled with energy.

"Well, color me cottontail!" she said. "You're the kittens who run the Purrfect Paw-tisserie! These muffins are so delicious, I could eat ten more."

Berlioz laughed, his nervousness falling away. "Good thing there are eleven more in the bag."

"I've been hearing the animals of Paris whisper about your café for weeks," Angelique told them. "But I've been so busy training, I never had time to stop in."

"I hope you'll come visit later," Marie said.

"If everything else on your menu is as good as these muffins, you bet I will," Angelique said. "Would you like to see the racecourse? I can give you a private tour."

There was a loud *chook-chook-chook* sound from above.

"A private tour!" Pouf squeaked as he jumped for joy, then nearly fell out of the tree. He caught his balance and scrambled to the ground.

"This is our friend Pouf," Toulouse told Angeliquc. "He's a huge fan."

Angelique smiled. "It's nice to meet you, Pouf. I was a huge fan of the Fantastic Rabbit Race, too. I remember the first time I met Edward Earsworth. I was so starstruck, my ears wouldn't stop shaking!"

"Is he the one who cheated?" Berlioz asked.

Angelique's brown eyes became sad. "Yes. But before he did that, he was an incredible racer. I really looked up to him." Angelique was quiet for a moment, then added, "I hope someday to be the kind of racer other animals look up to."

"You already are!" Pouf squealed, then ran behind the tree.

Angelique's smile came back. "Thank you! So I guess we should start the tour at the starting line. That's right over here."

Angelique showed them a line on the ground made of acorns, twigs, and leaves. From there, she led the kittens and Pouf along the rest of the racecourse. There were rocks to jump over, wooden gates to crawl through, and branches to shimmy under. Along the way, Berlioz noticed that other rabbit racers gave Angelique suspicious glances, and none of them spoke to her.

At a tree, the rabbits would have to climb in one hole in the trunk and out another. An enormous cream-colored hare was stretching his legs in front of the tree.

"Oh! Wow! Gosh!" Pouf whispered. "That's Yuri the Fury! He almost won last year!"

The hare glanced up when he heard his name and waved at them. "Hello, friends!"

"Hello!" Berlioz replied. He waved back. Toulouse, Marie, and Pouf all did, too.

Yuri looked over at Angelique . . . and his friendly expression disappeared.

 28

Angelique wasn't waving back. She was staring intensely at the tree trunk, almost as if she was ignoring the other racer on purpose.

"Hmmph," Yuri grumbled, then turned and hopped away.

After he'd gone, Angelique turned her attention back to the kittens and Pouf.

"Sorry," she said. "I was trying to figure out the fastest way into that hole. Sometimes I get lost in thought. What were you saying?"

"We were just saying hello to another racer," Berlioz said.

"I hope they said hello back," Angelique said. "They're not the friendliest bunch." She paused for a moment, looking hurt. Then she smiled and added, "Just wait until you see the first maze!"

The first maze was laid out along a stretch of tall grass and flowers. A small charcoal-gray dwarf rabbit was making her way out of the maze just as Angelique and her visitors were approaching.

"Hello, Mimi," Angelique said to the rabbit. "How'd you do in there?

"I was super-speedy," Mimi replied. "The race committee gnawed up some of the grass on the ground overnight, so it's nice and smooth. I hate when it's rough."

"Oh, I don't mind rough grass," Angelique said. "I'm actually superfast on grass that's ragged and full of weeds. That's what I'm used to."

Mimi was silent for a few moments,

twitching her nose. She seemed annoyed and offended. Finally, she just said, "All right, then. I'm off."

Like Yuri, Mimi sped away to another part of the racecourse.

"Well, *that* was awkward," Toulouse murmured to Marie. "It seems like Angelique doesn't always say the right thing."

"I noticed that, too," Marie murmured back. "If Mama were here, she'd show Angelique how to be more aware of her manners."

"Next up is the twisty tunnel!" Angelique announced, unaware of the kittens' whispering. As they followed her to the next stop on the tour, Pouf ran beside them, chattering every bit of Fantastic Rabbit Race trivia he knew.

Along the way, Berlioz noticed a group of other rabbits on the sidelines of the course. As soon as they spotted Angelique, they huddled close to one another and started talking softly.

But Angelique didn't notice at all.

"This is the toughest part of the race," she told them as she hopped up to the open end of a black tube. "It twists and turns, and when you're in there, it's so dark! You have to rely on your whiskers and your rabbit sense to know which way to go."

"A lot of luck helps, too," someone said from behind them.

Angelique, the kittens, and Pouf looked to see who it was.

"Oh! Wow! Gosh!" Pouf murmured

when he saw the shaggy, lop-eared
bunny. "That's Lucky McLop!"

"Good day to you, Lucky,"
Angelique said.

"That's Mr. McLop to you,"
the other bunny snorted, peering at
Angelique through messy bangs. "I
hear you've been acting rather high and
mighty around all of the other racers.

Your racing career might be taking off like a shooting star, but remember: the last rabbit to go from zero to hero that quickly was Edward Earsworth . . . and we all know what happened there."

Angelique looked confused. "I promise, I'm not high and mighty. I'm just me."

"Hmph," Lucky McLop said. "We shall see. Now if you'll excuse me, it's my turn to take a practice run in the tunnel."

With that, he bounded toward the tunnel entrance, his fluffy tail disappearing into the darkness.

"You're right," Berlioz said to Angelique. "The other racers aren't very friendly to you."

"It's okay," Angelique said, staring

into the tunnel. "It doesn't bother me. I'm just trying to focus on my racing."

Berlioz leaned in close to Toulouse. "Do you think all that ignoring really *does* bother her?"

Toulouse studied Angelique's face, then whispered, "Maybe. But it seems like sometimes, she ignores the others, too."

"Should we help?" Berlioz asked.

Toulouse thought hard for a few moments. "No. Remember what Pierre said about being good businesscats?"

"Right," Marie chimed in. "We don't want the other racers to think we're playing favorites."

Berlioz frowned. "I still think it's wrong for them to be so unfriendly to Angelique."

"I know you like to try to fix everything, Berlioz," Toulouse said. "But sometimes, you just can't—Oh! Look!"

A bright white moth fluttered past. Toulouse leapt for it, but missed. As it flew away, Toulouse abandoned their conversation and started chasing after it.

Berlioz turned to Marie.

"Is it really right to stay out of it if I could be doing something helpful that makes everyone feel welcome?" he asked.

Marie thought for a moment. "I'm sure someone else will step in, and you won't have to—Ahhh! It's back!"

The moth zipped in a circle around their heads, then flew off in another direction. Marie followed it, calling, "Mine! Mine! I'm going to catch it!"

 36

Berlioz watched her disappear around a bush.

"Thanks for the great talk, you two," he said sarcastically. Then he heaved a huge sigh, determined to do something for his new friend Angelique . . . even if that meant doing it on his own.

Chapter 3

The next day, the entire Paw-tisserie was filled with rabbit racers, hungry after their morning practice runs through the course. Marie was serving up carrot muffins as quickly as she could bake them.

"Looks like news about the Paw-tisserie is really *hopping* around," Toulouse said to Berlioz as they took in the scene. "I'd better go help Marie."

"And I'll go meet all these new customers," Berlioz said.

While Toulouse bounded over to the pastry case, Berlioz made his way among the tables. Yuri the Fury shared a croissant with Lucky McLop, chatting and laughing. Mimi the dwarf rabbit split a nut-berry tart with her chipmunk pit crew. A pair of white rabbits had pushed their chairs close together and were deep in conversation. Pouf sat by himself at a tiny table in the corner, watching everyone and flicking his tail with excitement.

The door to the café opened, and Angelique came in. She glanced around the room. When she realized that all the tables were filled, she hopped toward the pair of white rabbits, who had an empty seat next to them.

"Hi, Snowball and Frosty," Angelique said to them. They stopped talking and stared at her. "Is this seat taken?"

One of the rabbits reached out and put a paw on the empty chair. "Actually, it is. We're expecting another racer any minute now."

The other rabbit snickered a bit, but Angelique just said, "Okay. See you both at the race tomorrow."

She moved on to the next table, where another rabbit racer sat by herself with a cup of tea and a plate of muffins.

"Good morning," Angelique greeted the rabbit. "We haven't met yet. I'm

Angelique. Do you mind if I sit with you?"

The rabbit twitched her nose and narrowed her eyes at Angelique. "But we *have* met. Just yesterday. My name is Marshmallow, remember?"

"Oh, right! Sorry! There are so many new names and faces for me to keep track of!"

"Well, the rest of us have known one another our whole lives," Marshmallow said, tipping up her chin. Then she spread her plate and cup out so they took up all the space at the table. "I'm afraid there's no room here for anyone else."

Berlioz glanced at Pouf. "Angelique is trying to be friendly, but everyone is giving her the cold shoulder. That's not right."

"Go say something," Pouf said. "It's your café! You're the boss!"

Berlioz thought for a moment and said, "That's true, but . . . I don't want to make trouble. Pierre warned us against that."

"Okay, maybe next time," Angelique was saying to the rabbit at the table.

"But maybe there's some other way we can help her," Berlioz murmured.

Berlioz scurried over to Angelique and grabbed her paw. "Come sit at the piano," he told her. "I'm not using it right now, and if you pull down the keyboard cover, it makes a nice table. In fact, that's where I usually have my lunch!"

After Angelique sat down at the
piano stool, she said, "Thanks. I'm
honored to sit at your piano . . . just
don't ask me to play! I'm definitely more
of a racer than a musician."

Berlioz took a carrot muffin from
the pastry case and brought it back to
Angelique, who dug into it.

"I have to say, it bothers me that
the other racers aren't welcoming
you into the racing community," he
told her.

Angelique gulped down the last of
the muffin and scratched behind one of
her ears, thinking. "Well, this race has
been a tradition for a long time," she
finally replied. "Things have always been
done a certain way. The other rabbits

here all come from families where their parents, siblings, and relatives have also been racers. They go to special racing schools and practice on fancy tracks. I didn't do any of that. My family doesn't even like racing! I became a racer because I always loved to run. In backyards, over rooftops, through the parks of Paris . . . I'm a racer just like the others, but I guess they don't see me that way. That's why I want to win the Fantastic Rabbit Race! Maybe if I do, they'll finally accept me. So this is about more than just a trophy for me."

"*More than just a trophy . . .*" Berlioz repeated to himself. "Hmmm. You know, that's giving me an idea. I'll be right back!"

Berlioz found Toulouse and Marie in the kitchen area.

"I can't believe how busy we are because of this race," Toulouse said as he took a tray of puppy treats out of the oven.

"It's like we're the unofficial home of all the contestants!" Marie added as she sliced a loaf of birdseed baguette.

"I was thinking the same thing," Berlioz said. "So . . . what if the café offered extra prizes to the winner?"

"Oooh," Toulouse said, his eyes growing wide. "I could paint a portrait of this year's champion. . . ."

"And I could compose a song for her . . . or him," Berlioz added, then turned to his sister. "What about you, Marie? Maybe you could bake a special carrot cake."

Marie was silent as she considered that, swishing her tail and glancing toward Angelique at the piano.

"I don't know," she said. "I have a feeling you just want to do all this because you think Angelique will win. That's not fair to the other racers."

"What?" Berlioz exclaimed. "No! Of course not. I want to do it for whoever wins. It's good for the café!"

Marie sighed. "Let me think about it," she said, and marched off to the kitchen area.

Berlioz leaned over to whisper in Toulouse's ear. "Angelique is absolutely going to win. . . ."

"Berlioz!" Toulouse said, swatting at him playfully. "Marie is right. We shouldn't take sides."

"But it's true!" Berlioz insisted as he swatted back. He laughed and looked out at the customers . . . then noticed someone new.

There, next to the two white rabbits who wouldn't let Angelique sit with them,

them, was a gray-and-white rabbit Berlioz had never seen before. He wore a green scarf and big glasses.

Who was *that*?

Chapter 4

Berlioz, Toulouse, and Marie ran through the Luxembourg Gardens, eager to get to the Fantastic Rabbit Race track in time for the start of the qualifying round. The first three rabbits to cross the finish line that day would compete in the next day's final.

"Hurry!" Berlioz called to his brother and sister. "Most of the other racers have their families here to cheer them on, but Angelique doesn't have anyone! We need to be her substitute family!"

Toulouse suddenly stopped running. "Berlioz, wait. We just announced to everyone that the café is offering special prizes. Won't it seem unfair if we're cheering on Angelique?"

Berlioz and Marie stopped, too.

"I'm with Toulouse," Marie said. "It looks bad if we're rooting for her and not the other racers."

Berlioz thumped his tail on the ground and flattened his ears. "But we're Angelique's friends. She needs us. The rabbits aren't welcoming her into the racing community."

"*You're* the one who's really her friend," Marie said. "At least, so far."

Berlioz considered that for a moment. "You're right. She's *my* friend. So *I'm* going to do what I want. I want to be her substitute family today."

He bounded toward the thicket of trees that hid the racecourse from humans. When he found the secret entrance and crawled through, Marie and Toulouse followed him. On the other side, the area was filled with rabbits and other animals of all kinds. Squirrels, chipmunks, and birds watched from branches above.

The other racers were surrounded by family members giving out last-minute advice and encouragement.

"You get nice height on that leap over rock three!" one older rabbit said to a racer. "But make sure you keep your left paw pointing forward, not out."

"Okay, Dad," the racer said. "Left paw forward. Got it."

"Your hair's looking a little dull today," a fluffy-maned rabbit said as she combed another racing rabbit's unruly fur. "A good brushing will shine it up."

"Oh, Mama," the rabbit racer said, pushing the comb away. "Stop fussing!"

Berlioz spotted Angelique stretching her legs by herself in a far corner and scampered over to her. But Marie and Toulouse didn't follow. Berlioz glared at them as they started doing a lap around the area, waving to all the other racers.

Angelique's face brightened when she saw Berlioz. "Hi!" she exclaimed. "I'm so happy to see you!"

Berlioz turned his attention away

from his littermates and toward his new friend. "Are you nervous?" he asked her.

"A little," Angelique admitted. "But I don't have to win this race. I just have to finish in the top three. I want to save my energy for tomorrow, if I make it."

Angelique switched to stretching the other leg.

"That's a good stretch," Berlioz said. "Excellent form."

Angelique stopped, stared at Berlioz, and twitched her nose. "Uh . . . thank you?"

"You're welcome! I'm trying to give encouragement and suggestions. Like the other rabbits are getting from their families."

Angelique broke into a huge smile. "Oh, Berlioz. That means a lot. I've always wanted my own crew to pep me up before a race."

"Well, now you've got one," Berlioz offered, then cleared his throat and added, "You've got this, Angelique! We believe in you! Keep your fur out of your eyes! And . . . um . . . don't let your claws catch on anything!"

Angelique laughed. "Thank you, Berlioz! I feel pepped up already!"

"Maybe every rabbit racer should have a feline pep squad," someone behind them said. Angelique and Berlioz turned around. It was the gray-and-white rabbit with glasses and the green scarf. "Pardon me for eavesdropping. I was

just coming by to introduce myself to
Angelique. My name is Skip Hopper."

"Nice to meet you, Skip," Angelique
said. "Are you ready for the qualifying
race?"

Skip grinned. "I'm just here to do
my best. Plus, it's a chance to meet all
these racers I admire so much, like you.
Everyone seems a little scared by how

fast you are, and they say you're not friendly. But I think you're wonderful."

Angelique's nose and whiskers twitched. "They say *I'm* not friendly? But they're the ones who—"

Just then, a swan's trumpet sounded through the starting line area.

"That was the ten-minute warning," Skip said. "We'd better get to the starting line. Good luck to you!"

"You too!" Angelique replied, but he was already hopping away.

After Angelique left for the starting line, Berlioz found his littermates. Together, they made a plan. Toulouse and Marie would stand at different points along the course so they could cheer on every racer as they came through. Berlioz wanted to stand at the finish line, along with the other racers' families, to encourage Angelique in the final stretch.

"I've already started making up her song prize for Angelique if she wins," Berlioz said. *"Angelique, Angelique, faster than a lightning streak. . . ."*

"I like that," Marie said. "You could use other words that rhyme with her name. Like *unique*. And *technique*. And—"

"It's *my* song," Berlioz said with a little huff. "I have lots of my own ideas. And you didn't even want to root for Angelique."

"Fine," Marie muttered, looking hurt. "I was just trying to help." She turned to Toulouse. "Come on, let's go take our places for the race."

They scampered off, and Berlioz headed for the finish line on his own.

Pouf was already stationed above the racecourse, in a perfect spot in the perfect tree. He could see what was happening and could shout it out to everyone below.

Finally it was time to start. The swan let out two short trumpets and a single long one, and twenty rabbit racers were off.

Pouf's high voice called out minute-by-minute updates.

"They're headed toward the first water hole! Wow, it's wet! And deep! Deep and wet! Angelique is already in the lead and . . . oh, that's strange! Weird! Bizarre! That rookie racer Skip

Hopper is running around the water hole. He lost so much time! Okay, next up comes a mud pit!"

"Yay, Angelique!" Berlioz called, even though he knew she couldn't hear him yet.

Pouf started chittering again. "They're on a straight section now! Right through the grass! Oh, look at Angelique go! Yuri the Fury is right behind her. Lucky McLop, too. Skip Hopper is following. Go, go, go!"

Pouf rattled off a constant narration of the race as the rabbits went into the twisty tunnel and emerged, then went into the maze and out. Angelique stayed in the lead the whole time. At all the water holes and mud pits, Skip Hopper went *around* instead of *through*. Then, after

going through a tunnel or maze, he'd be right behind Angelique.

Finally the racers came into view on their way to the finish line. When he spotted Angelique in the lead, Berlioz started shouting the beginning of his song:

"Angelique! Angelique! Faster than a lightning streak!"

The cheer seemed to give Angelique a little burst of energy as she sped up and leapt across the finish line. Skip Hopper bounded across just seconds behind her. Lucky McLop finished third. Angelique, Skip, and Lucky were instantly surrounded by excited fans. Mimi the dwarf rabbit was next to complete the race. When she saw that Angelique had outrun her, Mimi's ears drooped with disappointment, and she hopped away from the celebration.

"Yay, Angelique!" Berlioz said, jumping up and down with excitement as Angelique came over. Her fur was wet, muddy, and rumpled, but she looked overjoyed.

"I think that was the fastest I've ever run a racecourse," Angelique said, catching her breath.

"But I don't understand," Berlioz said. "Why did Skip run around all the wet and messy parts of the race? How did he still finish second?"

"He must be really fast in the tunnels and mazes," Angelique said. "Every racer has their strengths and weaknesses."

Berlioz spotted Marie and Toulouse

as they arrived at the finish line area. Toulouse glanced over at Skip and his crowd and smiled.

Marie positioned herself at the finish line, continuing to cheer for each rabbit as he or she completed the race. Yuri the Fury was the last to come in, limping his way through the final stretch. He scowled when he saw that Angelique had placed first.

"Ugh!" Yuri exclaimed. "If I hadn't fallen and twisted my foot, I'm sure I would have beaten that newcomer!"

Berlioz thumped his tail on the ground, annoyed and frustrated. The other racers were still being unfair to Angelique. Also, why did Toulouse seem to be rooting for Skip?

All eyes and ears would now be on the big final event. Hopefully, Angelique would be able to repeat her victory. . . .

That would be the best way to prove everyone wrong.

Chapter 5

"Voilà!" Marie said. "May I present
to you the Race Day Deluxe Power
Breakfast!"

She proudly pushed a plate toward
Angelique, across the counter at the
Purrfect Paw-tisserie. Berlioz looked on
with anticipation.

Angelique admired the breakfast,
her brown nose twitching. There
was an extra-large carrot muffin, a

nut-berry tart, a spinach mini quiche, and some dandelion greens on the side.

"Thank you and . . . wowza!" Angelique said. "Power indeed!"

"It's been a huge hit this morning," Marie said.

She pointed to a sign that Toulouse had painted, advertising the breakfast for all racers and their supporters. The café was filling up quickly with animals wanting to eat before the championship race.

"Your café really *has* become the unofficial race headquarters," Angelique said. She sat down at a table and started digging into the food. Berlioz took a seat beside her.

"Are you nervous?" Berlioz asked Angelique.

"I'm always a little nervous," she replied between bites of quiche. "But I see that as a good thing. It gives me energy and focus. This delicious meal will help, too. Hey, Berlioz, since you volunteered to be my Fantastic Rabbit

Race family, could you lend me a paw with some strategy?"

"Of course!" Berlioz said enthusiastically.

"What do you think Lucky McLop's big weakness is, on the racecourse?"

Berlioz took a few moments to think.

"Pouf said he slipped on the grass after he ran through a mud pit," he finally offered.

"It's true!" Pouf exclaimed, appearing out of nowhere. "He was in second place! Then he went into a water trap! Then he came out! Skip got ahead of him! Lucky is slower when his feet are wet!"

"Hmmm, good to know," Angelique

said. "It sounds like Skip is the racer I have to worry about."

"He ran around the mud!" Pouf said. "And the water, too! Why did he do that? It doesn't make sense!"

"But somehow he made up the time in the tunnels and mazes," Berlioz added. "He definitely has a chance of winning."

"Looks like he's gotten a lot more popular since yesterday's race," Angelique said, nodding toward a corner table where Skip sat, surrounded by race fans eager to chat with him. A few feet away, Toulouse had set up an easel and was painting Skip's portrait.

Berlioz narrowed his eyes, jumped out of his chair, and bounded over to his brother.

"Hey!" Berlioz said. "I thought you weren't going to support any single racer because that was bad for the café!"

Toulouse sighed and put down his paintbrush. "Some chipmunks offered me a good deal on nuts for the kitchen in exchange for painting Skip's portrait. We could really use more nuts! Plus, I think Skip is just as great a racer as Angelique."

"I knew it," Berlioz said. "You're going to root for him, aren't you?"

"Well, *you're* rooting for Angelique. I'm just balancing you out! And why wouldn't I support Skip? Did you see how he made up time in the race?"

"I did," Berlioz admitted. "And I thought it was strange."

"Well, *I* thought it was awesome!" Toulouse said.

Berlioz let out a soft little growl at Toulouse, and Toulouse stuck out his tongue at Berlioz before he went back to painting. Berlioz sighed. Toulouse had a point about helping Skip. It was only fair, since *he* was helping Angelique.

Berlioz watched for a few moments, examining the portrait. Toulouse was filling in the green on Skip's green scarf with a small paintbrush. Then Berlioz noticed something on the canvas: there was a tiny bit of gold paint peeking out from behind the scarf.

"What's that?" Berlioz asked his brother, pointing to the gold paint.

"I'm not sure," Toulouse replied. "I just saw it, and I really liked the color."

"Chook-chook-chook." A high voice chittered from behind them. Berlioz turned to see Pouf perched on top of the piano, glaring at the squirrels surrounding Skip.

"So you're still an Angelique fan even though your friends are Team Skip now?" Berlioz asked.

"Of course!" Pouf squeaked. "Always! Forever! And ever and ever and ever—"

"Okay!" Berlioz said, laughing. "Glad to hear it." He hopped up onto the piano and whispered in the squirrel's ear. "There's something about Skip that just doesn't seem right. Have you noticed that?"

Pouf let out another *chook-chook-chook* and leaned down to examine Toulouse's painting. "Yes! Skip reminds me of someone! Can't figure out who!"

Two mice rushed out of Skip's fan crowd and approached Marie at the counter.

"Emergency!" one mouse called. "Stop what you're doing!"

The other mouse squeaked, "Skip would like a Race Day Deluxe Power Breakfast right away!"

"And a cup of lavender tea with milk and honey," the first mouse added.

"Sure," Marie said. "Coming right up."

"Hurry! Hurry!" the mice shouted.

"I'll make it as fast as I can," Marie replied, flattening her ears in annoyance.

"I'd better go help," Toulouse murmured to Berlioz as he put down his brush and dashed into the kitchen.

Berlioz studied the painting, and especially the gold blob. He looked over at Skip. There was no blob next to his scarf. But then Skip leaned forward to say something to a chipmunk . . . and there it was! It almost looked like a tiny key, hanging from a gold chain. Skip leaned back, and the key was gone.

After a few minutes, Marie and Toulouse came out from behind the counter pushing a cart filled with Skip's order. When they reached his table, the crowd of fans parted like a curtain to let them in.

"Thank you," Skip said, flashing a charming smile at the kittens. The two

mice excitedly jumped onto the wheels
of the cart and started climbing.

"We told Marie what you wanted!"
one exclaimed.

"Is it good? Are you happy?" the
other asked.

When they reached the top of the
cart, they both leapt onto the tray just as
Skip was bending down to take his first
sip of tea. It made the cup jiggle, which
made the tea splash . . . which made a
tiny drop slosh out of the cup, into the
air, and onto Skip's scarf.

Skip jumped up, frantically waving
his front paws.

"Aaaaaghhhh!" Skip cried. "*What
have you done!* Oh! Oh! Someone, get me a
napkin! Wipe it off! Quickly!" His ears

twitched and his whiskers quivered as he kept shouting, "Ew! Yuck! Ew! Yuck!"

Berlioz leapt forward and wiped off the drop of tea with his front paw. "All gone!"

"Thank you," Skip muttered, breathing heavily.

"Are you okay?" Berlioz asked.

"Yes, yes. I'm fine now." Skip turned to Marie. "I'm afraid I don't have an appetite anymore."

A jet-black rabbit named Coco, who was one of the race officials, climbed onto a table. She thumped a back foot several times on the wood.

"Everyone! Everyone!" she announced. "The championship running of the Fantastic Rabbit Race will start in fifteen minutes!"

There was an instant hustle and bustle throughout the café as everyone headed toward the exit.

"Here I go!" Angelique said, joining the crowd.

Pierre offered to stay behind and get everything ready for the postrace celebration.

"My heart's already racing. This is going to be amazing!" Marie exclaimed as she started to leave. "Hey! I made a rhyme, just like Berlioz!"

Toulouse laughed as he followed Marie out the door, but Berlioz paused. He ran back to the piano and quickly played out a melody, singing Marie's rhyme.

My heart's already racing . . . this is going to be amazing!

"That fits perfectly with the song you've been working on," Pierre remarked.

"It really does," Berlioz said. "Maybe that's the ending I needed."

But with the race about to begin, there was no time to try it out now . . .

 81

or to tell Marie she'd helped him figure out the song. Berlioz rushed out the door.

When he emerged into the alley, he spotted something strange: three rabbits huddled by the wall. It was Skip Hopper and the two white rabbits, Snowball and Frosty, who'd been disqualified in the first race. They were all whispering together.

"That seems odd," Berlioz murmured to himself. When the rabbits started hopping down the alley and toward the street, Berlioz followed them. They were still talking softly, so Berlioz couldn't hear what they were saying. He went into his lightest alley cat walk, the way his stepfather, Thomas O'Malley, had taught him. He knew this would get him close enough to eavesdrop without the rabbits noticing.

Berlioz slinked along, hiding behind carriages, tree trunks, lampposts, and anything else he came across. But the rabbits were always a few paces ahead of him, and Berlioz couldn't get within earshot.

When the rabbits reached the race starting line area, Skip was suddenly mobbed by more new fans. Berlioz couldn't keep up.

But he was as confused—and curious—as ever.

Chapter 6

"What's your favorite type of carrot, Skip?"

"Team Hopper! Team Hopper!"

"Skip, would you sign my paw?"

Skip's admirers were suddenly everywhere, and Berlioz lost sight of Frosty and Snowball. But then . . . there they were! The two rabbits stepped around to the other side of a tree. Berlioz crouched down and snuck closer, hiding behind the next tree over. He pointed both ears in the direction of the white rabbits and could hear them talking softly.

"Do you really think this key strategy will work again?" one of the rabbits asked the other.

"Why wouldn't it?" the other white rabbit replied.

Berlioz frowned. *Key strategy?*

The rabbits were snickering now. "I can't wait to see Angelique's face when Skip crosses the finish line first!" one said.

"Maybe then she'll understand that she never belonged here."

Berlioz started softly growling with anger. Before he even knew what he was doing, he burst from his hiding spot and let out a *mrrrrow-hissssss!*

The rabbits turned, startled, but when they saw only a dark gray kitten with a red bow, they started laughing. Berlioz puffed up his fur and opened his mouth to say something . . . but nothing came out.

"What's the matter?" one of the rabbits taunted. "Cat got your tongue?"

Both rabbits laughed again, louder this time. Berlioz dropped his tail between his legs and dashed off to find Marie and Toulouse.

"There you are!" Marie exclaimed when Berlioz came running up to them. "The race will be starting soon. I was thinking we could all stay together and try to run along with the racers. We'll be able to catch up when they go into the tunnels and mazes because we can run straight. I don't want to miss a second of this!"

"Good idea," Berlioz said. "But first, I have to tell you about what I just heard. There were these two rabbits. They sounded like they were planning something . . . and like they knew Skip was going to win. We have to find out what they're up to!"

"There's no time," Toulouse said. "Look!"

He pointed over at Angelique, who was already at the starting line, shaking out her back paws. Lucky McLop had just gotten into position, too. Skip pushed his way out of the crowd of fans to take his spot. Angelique didn't notice either of them. She stared straight ahead, focusing on the first part of the racecourse.

Two swans sounded the starting trumpets. *Honnnnnk!*

In a blur of motion, the three racers took off from the starting line as all the spectators cheered.

"Go, Lucky, go!" "You can do it, Skip!" "An-ge-lique!"

Angelique took the biggest leaps forward, but Lucky and Skip were both very fast as they darted across the first patch of grass and jumped over one big rock, then under a gate. Now it was a dash to reach the first water hole. Angelique sped right through it, kicking up a giant splash as she went. Lucky tried his best in the water, but he was much slower than Angelique. By the time he got to the other side, Angelique was several paces ahead of him.

Skip ran right up to the water's edge . . . then turned and ran right *around* the hole. This allowed Lucky to get a solid hold on second place.

When the three racers approached the first mud pit, the same thing happened. Angelique powered through, Lucky did his best, and Skip ran off the course in order to avoid the mud. Now he'd fallen even farther behind Angelique and Lucky.

"Why does he keep doing that?" Berlioz shouted to Marie and Toulouse as the three kittens hurried along the sidelines of the course.

"It's just part of his racing style!" Toulouse called back. "He's so cool!"

"Watch!" Marie added. "They're about to go into the first twisty tunnel!"

In went Angelique. Then Lucky. Then Skip. The kittens raced to where the tunnel let out.

After about a minute, everyone heard footsteps approaching the exit. Had Angelique held on to her lead?

Yes! There she was, smiling when she heard the cheers of the crowd.

More footsteps, coming right on Angelique's heels. Had Lucky made up time?

It was Skip! The crowd went wild, roaring with excitement.

"He really is fast in the tunnels," Toulouse said, clearly impressed. Berlioz rolled his eyes.

Angelique glanced over her shoulder and looked surprised to see Skip right there. She took a deep breath and sped up even more as she jumped over a rock, crawled under a gate, and practically dove into another water hole. By this time, Lucky had emerged from the first tunnel, and although he was clearly running as fast as he could, he kept slipping on the wet grass and muddy parts of the racecourse.

But he'd managed to pass Skip, who had decided once again to run all the way around anything that was wet or dirty.

"Go, Angelique!" Berlioz shouted.

Angelique quickly and gracefully crawled through the tree with the hole in it, then focused on the entrance to the first maze. Lucky was at least ten paces behind her, and Skip was even farther back.

"I don't think Lucky or Skip can make up the time," Berlioz said.

"Anything can happen!" It was Pouf, above them in the tree. "Angelique could fall! Or get lost in the maze! That's why the race is so exciting until the end!"

Angelique waved at them, smiling, as she entered the maze. Lucky saluted his fans as he went in a few moments later. Then Skip did a showy kind of lcap-and-twirl before he disappeared through the opening.

"Now we wait!" Pouf chittered. "I hate waiting! Wait, wait, wait! Blech!"

Berlioz, Toulouse, and Marie sprinted to the maze's exit.

"I hope she remembers the way," Berlioz said.

Suddenly, a flash of brown fur burst out of the maze's exit. It was Angelique!

She was followed instantly by a flash of gray and white. Skip. Close enough to grab at Angelique's tail.

"I can't believe it!" Toulouse exclaimed. "He keeps catching up! Running around the water holes and mud pits must be part of his strategy!"

Berlioz's ears perked up. *Strategy?* Then, suddenly, his eyes went wide with a brainstorm.

"Pouf!" Berlioz called to the squirrel above them. "Remember you said that Skip's portrait reminded you of someone?"

"Yes! Still bugs me!" Pouf flicked his tail, which was extra puffy with excitement, back and forth.

"Was it Edward Earsworth, by any

chance?" Berlioz asked. "The cheating racer who got expelled?"

Pouf froze. His tail stopped twitching. His round eyes grew as big as marbles.

"Edward! Yes! But he had a pink nose! Skip has a black nose! Glasses, too! But they could be brothers!"

Berlioz called to his littermates. "Toulouse! Marie! Quick, follow me!"

"Why?" Marie asked.

"I know how Skip is making it through the mazes and tunnels so fast!" he said. "He's cheating!"

"He wouldn't do that," Toulouse said.

"I know you think he's cool," Berlioz said. "But you have to trust me. I found out what's really going on, and I'll explain it on the way. Please, just come!"

Berlioz turned and ran off toward the finish line. Marie and Toulouse looked at each other, confused . . . then started chasing their brother.

Chapter 7

Angelique darted through another hole in another tree and out the other side, then started crawling under a web of branches. Skip slipped through the tree as well, leaping onto the grass so that he avoided a small puddle left by the rain. He lost a few precious seconds that way.

They went through another maze, and then another tunnel. Both times,

Skip came out much closer to Angelique than when he went in.

Up ahead, Angelique was slowing down. Everyone could see she was exhausted, but Skip didn't look tired at all.

There was just one sharp turn left before a straight section of the racecourse that led to the finish line. Angelique took the turn tightly, but Skip took it even tighter, and now they were ear to ear as they ran.

A moment later, Skip took a giant stride and blew by Angelique.

"No! Go! No! Go!" Pouf chittered from above. "Skip's going to win!"

Now the finish line was five feet away . . . four . . . three . . . two . . . one . . .

But he stopped cold right before his front foot crossed the line. Skip stood frozen, staring up ahead with a look of horror on his face. His nose and whiskers twitched uncontrollably.

Thump-thump-whoosh.

Angelique breezed past Skip and crossed the finish line, sliding into a huge puddle of dirty, muddy water.

Splash!

The crowd burst out into cheers and rushed to surround Angelique.

"She did it!" Pouf called. "She won!"

"Yes!" Berlioz shouted. He was standing on the other side of the finish line, holding an empty bucket.

Toulouse and Marie stood next to him, empty buckets in their paws as well.

All three kittens admired the mucky puddle they'd just created by dumping water on the ground beyond the finish line.

"I have to admit," Marie said to Berlioz, "your idea to make a puddle here, where it wouldn't interfere with the actual race, was pretty smart."

"Your idea to borrow the buckets

from that park building was great, too," Berlioz said.

"Don't forget my suggestion to get the water from the nearest fountain!" Toulouse reminded them.

"High paws all around for us kittens!" Berlioz said, and all three of them laughed.

Angelique hopped over, a group of fans in tow. "That was a truly fantastic rabbit race! But why did Skip suddenly stop and freeze like one of the park statues?"

Berlioz glanced over at Skip, who was still standing, motionless, just before the finish line. He looked defeated and embarrassed, especially as Lucky McLop sped past him through the puddle to finish in second place.

Berlioz turned to Angelique and said, "Long story short, Skip Hopper is not who he says he is."

Now Skip thumped his hind foot nervously on the ground. "Oh yes? And who would I be, if I'm not me?"

"Edward Earsworth!" Berlioz cried.

Lots of gasps, tweets, meows, barks, and squeaks rose from the spectators.

"Here's a bit of rabbit racing trivia I learned from my friend Pouf," Berlioz announced to the crowd. "Edward Earsworth was famous for refusing to get wet or muddy. Even a little drop of . . . say . . . *tea* on his clothes would make him upset. So I thought, if Edward was running this race in disguise, a giant patch of wet goo like this one might stop him from crossing the finish line. And I was right!"

Angelique turned to Skip, then hopped closer to examine his face. "Is all this true?"

"No . . . Of course not . . . I . . . How dare . . ." he muttered. Then he breathed in a huge sigh, shook his glasses off his face, and wiped black paint off his nose. Underneath, it was pink.

"You know what else?" Berlioz continued. "He has a key around his neck! He was using that to cheat in the race." Berlioz turned to Skip. "I overheard your friends talking about your 'key strategy,' and then I figured it out when I remembered some more of Pouf's trivia: Edward Earsworth cheated by using a special key to get into secret short, straight passageways underneath the tunnels and mazes. It let him get through them much faster."

Angelique turned to Skip. "Is that true? Were there secret passageways under the racecourse?"

Skip sighed. "Yes. They've been there for years. My friends Snowball and Frosty asked me to come back and use them, to make sure you didn't win. But I had to come up with a disguise."

"But why wouldn't they want her to win?" Marie asked. "What did she ever do to you? Or anyone?"

"It's more like what she *never* did!" Edward said with a snort. "Angelique never went to racing school! She never practiced on proper tracks! It's not right that she should win. Plus, she's not very friendly and seems too full of herself." Edward turned to his friends. "Right?"

Snowball and Frosty laughed. "Right!" Snowball agreed.

"Who does she think she is?" Frosty added.

Berlioz glanced at Angelique, who looked deeply hurt. Then he puffed up his fur and flattened his ears, taking two big steps toward Edward.

"Who does she think she is?" Berlioz echoed. "She's herself! She's fast and she loves to run! Just because she took a different path to get here doesn't mean she's not a real racer." Now Berlioz turned to Snowball and Frosty. "My question is who do you think *you* are, believing that cheating is okay?"

"You can't be proud of anything you get from cheating," Marie added. "That's what our Mama always says, and now I understand what she means."

Snowball and Frosty opened their mouths to say something, but nothing came out. Instead, they ran over and huddled behind Edward.

Toulouse narrowed his eyes at Edward and shook his head. "I can't believe I thought 'Skip Hopper' was so amazing . . . when it turns out you're anything but."

Edward just looked down at his feet.

Berlioz glanced out over the crowd. "You know what's also not okay? All you racers being so unfriendly to Angelique."

Yuri the Fury hopped forward. "Us unfriendly to *her*? She's the one who's been unfriendly to us!"

"We're not like Edward and his friends," added Lucky. "I think a great rabbit racer is a great rabbit racer, no matter how she got that way. But she almost never says hello, or waves, or even remembers our names. Sometimes she just ignores us."

"And sometimes she just brags about herself!" Mimi the dwarf rabbit chimed in.

Angelique's jaw dropped open. "Is that what you think? I do tend to focus too much on racing, and then I forget to pay attention to what's going on around me. I'm so sorry if I seemed rude. I just want to fit in and be friends with you all, but I'm not very good at that kind of thing."

Yuri, Lucky, and Mimi exchanged a guilty glance, their noses twitching.

Then Yuri smiled softly and said, "I remember when I was new to racing. I felt the same way. All I thought about was speed and not so much about the other rabbits."

"We should have tried harder to get to know you," Mimi added, "instead of judging you so quickly."

"Agreed," said Lucky.

"I should have tried harder, too," Angelique said. "Can we start over, without all these misunderstandings?"

Lucky smiled. "I can't speak for

everyone else, but I know *I* would
like to."

"Me too!" Mimi added, and Yuri
nodded along.

Suddenly, all the other rabbit
racers—and their families—came up to
congratulate Angelique and introduce
themselves.

Meanwhile, the race officials were
huddled together, whispering. Coco
stepped out of the huddle to make an
announcement:

"Edward Earsworth! Frosty!
Snowball! We ban you from the Fantastic
Rabbit Race . . . forever!"

Everyone turned to see Edward's
reaction. But he, and the two white
rabbits, were gone.

Chapter 8

It was biggest carrot cake anyone at the Purrfect Paw-tisserie had ever seen.

There were three layers, all frosted in fresh cream cheese. Toulouse had used orange icing to paint garden designs all around the sides. The top of the cake was decorated with a pair of bunny ears made by one of the blackbirds.

The café was practically bursting with animals of all kinds, excited to celebrate Angelique's win. Duchess and

Thomas O'Malley, along with many
of the kitties from Alley Cat Parlor at
Madame Bonfamille's home, had also
joined the party.

Marie, Toulouse, and Berlioz pushed
the cake cart out into the café together
while everyone cheered. Angelique stood
on top of a table, thumping her back
paw excitedly.

"Thank you!" she said, wiping a

tear from her eyes. "I couldn't have done it without the support of all my fans. Especially my 'racing family,' you kittens!"

Berlioz, Marie, and Toulouse smiled at one another, purring.

Once everyone had a piece of cake, the race official Coco announced, "To Angelique! Our Fantastic Rabbit Race champion!"

"To Angelique!" everyone echoed. "Our champion!"

"Yes, cheers to Angelique!" cried someone from within the crowd. "The fastest rabbit and most natural racer I've ever seen!"

All heads turned, eager to see who'd spoken.

Edward Earsworth stepped forward,

up to the table where Angelique stood. Everyone at the Paw-tisserie gasped.

"I'll be gone in a moment, I promise," Edward said. "But I need to say something to Angelique."

He turned to her.

"I'm truly sorry about cheating in the race. I'm sorry I ever felt you didn't deserve to win. That was wrong."

Angelique stared at him. "What changed your mind?"

Edward glanced at Berlioz and said, "I've been thinking about how you, Berlioz, knew something wasn't right. You were determined to figure out the truth. I've never had anybody stick by me the way you stuck by Angelique, even when I was a champion. I was never the kind of rabbit, or racer, who deserved that kind of loyalty. But that's the heart of what the Fantastic Rabbit Race stands for: a rabbit doing their best, and inspiring others to do the same."

Angelique smiled. "You sound a lot like the Edward Earsworth I used to look up to, back when I was just a young bunny. I liked how determined he was. Maybe you can use that determination for something else now. Something positive."

Edward grinned. "I'm *determined* to find out."

"I'll never be a 'Skip Hopper' fan again," Toulouse said to Edward. "But if Edward Earsworth does something fantastic in an honest way . . . you can count on me to cheer you on."

"Thank you, Toulouse," Edward replied. "Perhaps I'll even do something that inspires you to paint a new portrait of me. The *real* me . . ."

"Isn't it time to eat the cake?" Pouf said, jumping onto the piano. "The cake! Yum, yum! Delicious! Now!"

"Yes!" Angelique said, offering a piece of cake to Edward. "Everyone should eat!"

Marie turned to Berlioz. "Are you going to sing your song prize?"

"Actually, I could use your help with that," he replied.

"Oh, I would love to sing it with you!" Marie exclaimed.

"I was hoping you'd . . . um . . . finish it with me first," Berlioz said. "Remember that rhyme you came up with? It fit in really well with the song. Do you have ideas for any more?"

Marie booped Berlioz on the nose with her paw.

"You silly," she said. "I always have ideas. All you had to do was ask!"

"I'm sorry it took me so long," Berlioz said. "When I saw how unfair it was that the rabbit racers weren't giving Angelique a chance, I realized I was also being unfair by not giving *you* a chance to write songs with me."

"Better late than never," Marie told her brother. "Come on, show me what you have so far."

As they headed over to the piano, Toulouse finished serving the cake. Every time someone told him how delicious it was or how much they liked the racetrack decoration, he purred a little louder.

Once everyone was done eating, Marie jumped on top of the piano.

"We have one final part of the celebration," she announced.

Berlioz made sure his tail was swept out behind him, adjusted the red bow on his collar, stretched out his fingers . . . and relaxed, ready to have fun.

He played the first chords as he and his sister started to sing the tune they'd written together:

My heart's already racing!
This is going to be amazing!
Oh Angelique, Angelique,
She's faster than a lightning streak
Watch her dash across the sky

See her hop and leap so high
She's the rabbit I wish I could be
Honest and serious
But wild and free
Angelique, Angelique,
There's no bunny like her
She's completely unique!

As Berlioz played and sang with Marie, Toulouse danced in a circle around them, swishing his tail to the bouncy beat. The littermates looked out onto the rest of the café and felt how exciting it all was: whom they'd met, what they'd learned, and what else might be possible at the Purrfect Paw-tisserie.

Whatever it was, the three kittens would pounce on it together.

Jennifer Castle is the author of over a dozen books for kids and teens, including the Butterfly Wishes series and American Girl's Girl of the Year: Blaire books. She lives in New Paltz, New York, with her family, which includes five cats, and, often, a few rescued foster kittens, who are all likely planning their own creature café when the humans aren't looking.

Sydney Hanson is a children's book illustrator living in Sierra Madre, California. Her illustrations reflect her growing up with numerous pets and brothers in Minnesota, and her love of animals and nature. She illustrates using both traditional and digital media; her favorites are watercolor and colored pencil. When she's not drawing, she enjoys running, baking, and exploring the woods with her family. To see her latest animals and illustrations, follow her on Instagram at @sydwiki.